A Day of Surprises

To Baptist, Manon, and Quentin.
V. T.

*Thank you, thank you, thank you, a thousand times and again
thank you to Alexis, Bâ-Lé, Carine, Clément, Damien, Élodie, Élise,
Emeline, Éric, Frédéric, Inès, Julien, Ludovic, Marietta, Olivier,
Romain, and Vincent!*
V. T.

Published in 2009 by Windmill Books, LLC
303 Park Avenue South Suite # 1280, New York, NY 10010-3657

Adaptations to North American edition © 2009 Windmill Books
Copyright © 2006 Editions Milan, 300 rue Léon Joulin - 31101 Toulouse Cedex 9, France.

CREDITS:
Author: Amélie Sarn
Illustrator: Virgile Trouillot
A concept by Frédéric Puech and Virgile Trouillot based on an idea from Jean de Loriol.
Copyright © PLaneTnemo

Publisher Cataloging Information

Sarn, Amélie
        A day of surprises / Amélie Sarn ; illustrations by Virgile Trouillot.
               p. cm. – (Groove High)
        Summary: The Groove High students deal with the fun and embarrassment
of school parents' day, including a visit from the famous choreographer Philippe
Kauffman, whose son Ed is a student at Groove High.
        ISBN 978-1-60754-209-4. – ISBN 978-1-60754-210-0 (pbk.)
ISBN 978-1-60754-211-7 (6-pack)
        1. Dance schools—Juvenile fiction   2. Parent and child—Juvenile fiction
3. Boarding schools—Juvenile fiction   [1. Dance schools—Fiction   2. Parent and
child—Fiction   3. Boarding schools—Fiction   4. Schools—Fiction] I. Trouillot,
Virgile   II. Title   III. Series
        [Fic]—dc22

Manufactured in the United States of America

Groove High

Amélie Sarn

A Day of Surprises

Illustrations by Virgile Trouillot

Skyview Books

an imprint of

WINDMILL BOOKS
New York

Me, I'm Zoe. I'm 14 years old and I'm following my dream: to go to Groove High to become a choreographer!

Vic: My best friend. Beautiful, blonde, and always on the cutting edge of fashion, and super fun to be around.

Lena: Athletic, rebellious, but also very disorganized! Paco, her crazy pet chameleon, is always in her pocket.

Tom: Very cool, but also very clumsy. He is crazy in love with Vic, who is not interested in him at all.

Ed: A little cold and mysterious at first glance, but actually a very nice guy and a talented dancer!

Philippe Kauffman: My idol! A great choreographer, he directs the Kauffman Academy, a school that rivals Groove High.

Miss Myer: My mother. She always tries to be my best friend, and this can be very annoying.

Table of Contents

Explosion at Rehearsal

"**Y**ou're nothing! No one! Less than nothing! Forget it, Tom! You'll never get anywhere!"

Tom stands on the stage. Vic continues her attack:

"Frankly, I wonder how you were even accepted to a dance school as prestigious as Groove High. Who did you convince to let you in? You can't even hold an arabesque for more than two seconds."

Lena and I just watch and listen. We're used to hearing Vic criticize Tom, but this time it's worse than usual.

Oops, sorry. I'm just going on and on and I haven't even introduced anyone. I'll start with Vic.

Vic is my best friend. She is blonde, beautiful, and

an amazing dancer. We've known each other since we were seven years old. We met at the Marie Court School of Ballet. Since then, we've been inseparable. But this doesn't mean we don't fight. We were all accepted to Groove High this year. Yes, you heard me correctly. This is Groove High, the famous dance school run by the world-renowned ballerina, Iris Berrens.

Now on to poor Tom. He is the nicest boy on Earth, but also the most klutzy. He's very funny and has a gift for doing impressions. Also—unfortunately for him—he is crazy in love with Vic. But he's not her type at all. She's much more into good-looking guys with a great sense of fashion. Preferably older, too. Tom is thirteen, maybe fourteen, and he looks it. There's no hope of Vic ever returning his feelings. But Tom is stubborn. It's not easy to discourage him, and he is always waiting for a chance to play the white knight for Vic. And I have to say, she takes advantage of this.

We met Lena our first day of auditions for Groove High—the same day we met Tom. She's dynamic, the kind of girl who knows how to take charge. She always wears a sweater, cargo pants, and a bandana around her head so she doesn't have to do her hair. She never has time for that, because she's always dealing with Paco, who loves to be pampered. Vic and I share a room with Lena, which means we also share a room with Paco. Can you imagine sharing a room with someone whose favorite activity is eating dried locusts? You guessed it, Paco isn't a person. He's a chameleon. And pets are strictly prohibited in the dorms, so Paco spends a lot of time hiding. Lena has installed a terrarium in the bathroom, but if there's a surprise inspection, she hides him in the closet. Don't worry, we make sure he gets out often for fresh air. And sometimes we give him baths. Which he loves.

Then there's me. Zoe Myer. I have strawberry blonde hair (not red, as some annoying people

like to say) and freckles on my nose (which I hate—my nose *and* my freckles).

Getting back to the story: Lena, Vic, and I are in the dance hall watching (for the fiftieth time this week) the show Tom has prepared for Parents' Day. Last Thursday, with eight days left till the end of the semester, Iris Berrens asked the group if anyone wanted to create a show to welcome the parents. Without thinking, Tom raised his hand. I wonder what went through his head! The truth is, Tom's a barely average dancer. He's far from the level of Vic or Kim, for example. And, sorry to say, he's short on originality, which Lena has a truckload of. I think he just hasn't quite found himself.

Iris Berrens was just as surprised as I was, but she accepted Tom's offer with pleasure.

"I'm delighted that you want to rise to this challenge, Mr. Muller!" she congratulated him with her usual coolness.

At the time, this honor went right to Tom's head. He didn't even notice Kim and her group whispering nasty things behind his back. (You haven't met Kim yet. Oh, she's just charming. Always there with kind words of "encouragement!")

However, as soon as we came out of class, Tom realized that he might've made a mistake. So he asked for our help. It's no surprise that I was the one who did his choreography. Vic and Lena acted as advisers.

The sequence Tom will perform is a mixture of tap dance, modern jazz, and hip-hop. I don't want to brag, but it's original, lively, and perfectly timed. It should, in my opinion, be a perfect dance for Parents' Day.

The only problem is that Tom can't get anything done. He's as stiff as a board, and, worse, he keeps tripping over his own feet. It's a mess. And every

step he takes is worse than the one before.

No wonder Vic's so annoyed.

"Where did you take your classes before Groove High, Tom?" Vic snaps. "Circus school?"

Now she has gone too far. Tom does not deserve this. To be fair, Vic hasn't been herself for the past few days. She's always a little sensitive, it's true, but lately it seems she's been getting up on the wrong side of the bed.

Tom stops. He looks at us like a lost puppy. It seems like he'll collapse at any second. But this doesn't stop my friend.

"Seriously, Tom," she says without pausing, "you're as awkward as a robot in a sci-fi spoof."

Confused and defeated, Tom leaves the stage. Vic raises her eyebrows. She looks at us.

"What's his problem?"

I shake my head. Lena gestures to me that she's going to go find Tom backstage. Good luck.

Vic stares at me with her wide open blue eyes. She doesn't get it. Vic always has a hard time realizing when she's out of line. She doesn't mean to be nasty; in fact, she has a heart of gold. She's always there for me, and she's the first to defend anyone who's weaker than she is. With Tom, it's different. He is so in love with her that he usually behaves like a doormat. But it has never gone this far before. I wonder what's been upsetting her so much these past few days. Whatever it is, Tom is paying for it.

"Vic, why were you so hard on him? He doesn't deserve to be treated like that! He's already super stressed out, and you're only making it worse!"

Vic presses her lips together. She hates to be lectured. Especially when she knows she deserves it. I try to avoid doing it if I can. Today, I'm aware that I'm going into a hungry tiger's cage. Vic's face is taut, her cheekbones more prominent than ever, her eyes shooting daggers.

"Everyone is annoying me!" she explodes. "And that includes you, Zoe! Actually, you're annoying me more than anyone. I thought friends were supposed to support each other!"

With this, she turns on her heel and marches out the door.

What happened? There were four of us in the room, and in less than two minutes, I find myself all alone. Alone with Vic's accusation. Why would she say I'm not supporting her? Obviously I've missed something, but what? I mentally yell for help. I try to think back.

"Zoe, are you there?"

The door that Vic has just slammed opens again. It's Ed, and he looks completely freaked out. His face is paler than ever.

"The parents are arriving!" he cries.

Parents' Day Nightmare

Ed is upset.

He doesn't live on campus like us. Instead, he lives with his father, the famous choreographer Philippe Kauffman, and his little brother, Kevin, a total pest, in a large apartment in the city center. Ed is a lonely, quiet boy, but through a combination of circumstances, he became our friend. Now there are five of us who make up the Groove Team: Tom, Vic, Lena, Ed, and me! We've even created our own indie magazine, *Groove Zine*, where we publish school news and gossip.

But I must confess. The reason I first befriended Ed is not very noble. I wanted a chance to be introduced to his father. My dream is to become a choreographer, and Philippe Kauffman has always inspired me. I am a huge fan. I even have a fat notebook packed with photos of him and his performances. Now that I know Ed, I actually like him for who he is. As a friend, he is absolutely awesome. But I still really want to meet his father. And now, with a little luck, it won't be long . . .

You probably realize that the long-awaited Parents' Day has arrived. Tom's performance? He goes on in less than half an hour. Is there any chance that he's improved in this short time? No!

"I ran all the way from home," Ed explains, trying to catch his breath. "I wanted to arrive before my father and brother."

Ed is tense. He has not been following the relaxation advice of our yoga teacher, Khan. (Who is, by the way, the best, the coolest, the most fun, most knowledgeable teacher in any school. Does it sound like I adore him? I do!)

Even though we've never talked about it, I think Ed and his father have problems. Here's a clue. Ed chose to audition at Groove High instead of the Kauffman Academy, the school his father runs.

Maybe Ed is sick of seeing his own father week after week in celebrity magazine photos. I can understand that. There's more. Philippe Kauffman is known not only for his genius as a choreographer, but also for his dazzling charm. He's always out on the town attending parties with other famous people. I hear he doesn't like to miss any. All this doesn't seem to impress Ed, but I'm amazed. If I were in Ed's shoes, I'd be so proud! I wouldn't let people forget that I was Philippe Kauffman's daughter. Especially since my parents are . . . well, you'll see.

Anyway, if I can support Ed, and at the same time get to meet my absolute idol, I won't complain.

"Well, are you coming?" Ed asks impatiently.

"Yes!"

It is nine o'clock when Ed and I arrive in the entrance hall of the freshman dorm. Angie and Clarisse—Kim Vandenberg's two obedient

followers—are standing there.

I haven't really told you about Kim yet. You're better off not knowing. She's selfish, sneaky, jealous, heartless, and rude. And she's also cowardly and hypocritical. Angie and Clarisse follow her every command, so she is always able to stay cool and collected. For example, if she has a sudden desire for sushi, she sends them scurrying downtown to order some and bring it back immediately. Her whole idea of friendship is bizarre.

Kim has a brother. He's a junior and his full name is Luke "The Flirt" Vandenberg. He and his friend Zachary run the Capoeira Club. Its members practice a combination of Brazilian martial arts and dance. Luke is a complete show-off. He also thinks he's quite a Don Juan. He changes girlfriends every week. Vic has a huge crush on him, for reasons I can't understand. I also don't understand why he calls me "Carrot Top" every time he sees me. (Did I mention that my hair is strawberry blonde?) Luke Vandenberg is good for one thing: he is good for getting on my nerves!

I look for Kim so I can avoid her, but I don't see her anywhere. I know her parents like trendy restaurants. Maybe they've already left to take her out to the newest sushi place near school.

Now that I'm looking, I realize Vic's not here, either. Where can she be? Is she still sulking? I hope not. Not on a day like today.

Tom is probably getting dressed. At least I hope so. Or maybe he's hiding. And where is Lena? Oh, here she comes, running down the hall. Huh? What is she wearing?

She has on a navy blue pleated skirt, a white blouse, polished black flats, and she has even removed the ever-present bandana from her head! Has someone abducted the real Lena?

She stops in front of the glass door to glance at her reflection. She must've dressed very quickly, because she still looks a little disheveled. But still, I hardly recognize her! She's probably playing some kind of joke on her parents. That must be it. What a hilarious idea!

Iris Berrens, our director, and Khan, our yoga teacher—the teacher who is the best, the coolest, the most fun, most—oh, I already told you? Sorry, but I can't help myself when I think of him! Anyway, Iris and Khan are both here. Iris Berrens approaches the front door. Here we go! Parents are coming!

In a crazy rush, which reminds me of a bunch of little kids being let out for recess, our parents flood into the hall.

"Zoe! My baby!"

I am suddenly crushed, pulverized, suffocated in my mother's arms, then my father's, and then my mother's again.

"Zoe! My baby!"

"Hi!" I say. You'd think we hadn't seen each other in two months. Come to think of it, it's been exactly two months since they've seen me.

Hands on hips, my father eyes sweep the room.

"It's beautiful here! I've only seen pictures, and it's more elegant than I imagined."

My mother applauds.

"Yes, it's ultra cool! You must be having an awesome time."

I think I forgot to tell you about my mother. How can I describe her? See, she really wants to know all about what she calls "the youth culture." She says this is a way for us to stay close. In reality, it's a way for her to try to be a teen herself! You'll hear her talking like a teenager, using slang like "ultra cool" and "awesome." Today, for example, she is wearing pink sneakers with yellow laces, tight jeans, and a top that shows her bare midriff. My father and I worked really hard to convince her not to have her belly button pierced.

"So, Darling, show us your school! We want to see everything!" my father exclaims.

"Totally," my mother adds. "And I want to meet all your teachers and your director. She is so famous! And her love story is so sad! Oh! Do you think I could ask for her autograph?"

I try to stay calm. I take a deep breath, and then I exhale just as slowly. I learned this in yoga class

from Khan, the best, most . . . okay, okay, you already know.

It's true that Iris Berrens had a romance that ended tragically. If you know anything about the dance world, you've probably already heard of it. It made newspaper headlines for several weeks in a row. Alexx Berrens, the famous choreographer, died at the height of his career in a motorcycle accident. Iris and Alexx, Alexx and Iris . . . it was the love story of the century. They had almost outdone Romeo and Juliet. Alexx wrote for Iris, Iris danced for Alexx. But Alexx Berrens died and Iris, left all alone and inconsolable, stopped dancing. She disappeared from sight completely for a while. And then she created our school with Khan: Groove High.

I can completely imagine my mother heading over to Iris Berrens and bursting out with a question like "Do you miss your husband?" I know it sounds ridiculous, but it's just the kind of embarrassing thing my mother would do. If I have to baby sit my mother all day, I'll be exhausted!

"Oh, pardon me."

My father has just bumped into a huge ficus tree

in the hall and managed to tip the pot over. Whoa! I just manage to catch the plant by a branch and keep it from crashing to the floor. Now that you know about my mother, I should tell you a little about my father. He is the nicest man on Earth, but he is extremely clumsy. Ten times worse than Tom. I'll have to keep an eye on him, too. This day is going to be a lot of work. Suddenly, something crosses my mind.

"Hey, Mom, do you know where Vic's parents are?"

"Oh, the poor darling," she says. "Her parents couldn't come."

I frown. I begin to understand why Vic has been so irritable. I'm sure she's upset that her parents aren't coming to see her. But why didn't she just tell me?

"Something came up last minute," my father says. "They called this morning to ask us to give Vic a kiss for them."

Last minute? So Vic didn't know they weren't coming. It's still a mystery why she's acting so strange. And now I have to tell her the bad news. Given her mood the past few days, she won't take this well. Anyway, where is Vic? Why hasn't she come down to welcome her parents? They're not here, but she didn't know they wouldn't show up. I don't get it.

"My deeeeeeeeear Iris! It is always a pleasure."

The squealing voice sounds like a seagull. It belongs to a tall man, dressed entirely in white, who is waving his long arms as he greets Iris. Next to him is a little blond boy, who is jumping up and down and turning his head excitedly from one thing to the next. This is Kevin, Ed's little brother, aka "the brat."

Meaning the man in white is . . . my heart beats faster . . . Philippe Kauffman? I'm beginning to have trouble breathing.

Iris Berrens, always very severe, tilts her head toward him without smiling. She seldom smiles, except when she's with Khan.

"Hello, Philippe," she replies primly. "Welcome to Groove High."

Philippe! She called him Philippe! That means it's him! I'm on the verge of fainting. Only a few steps separate me from the fabulous Philippe Kauffman!

"Oh, excuse me! I'm so sorry! I . . ."

Dad! He's trying to use the water fountain in the hall, and of course he's managed to spill a cup of water on Khan, who is chatting with some of the parents. I'm so embarrassed!

"Wait, wait!" my mother cries, pulling a napkin from her purse. The napkin is black and has a skull on it. She bends close to Khan and eagerly dabs his jacket. I want to die!

Khan smiles, showing his beautiful teeth. I told you he is the best teacher. He's from India. His real name is so long and hard to pronounce that we just call him Khan. Now he speaks in his warm, kind voice as usual.

"Zoe, you haven't introduced me to your parents," he says, resting his bright black eyes on me.

I'm mortified. How does he know these are my parents?

"Yes, Darling, introduce us to your teacher!" Mom says.

Before I have time to open my mouth, she interjects:

"This place is so totally swee-eet. The kids must have a rockin' time here."

"Yes," Khan says, "I think they have a lot of fun. Anyway, I hope . . ."

If I could, I would disappear into thin air. If Parents' Day is a school tradition, I'm going to protest and demand that this tradition comes to an end.

"I think it's very important to meet our students' parents," Khan goes on. "And for them to experience the place where their children live during the school year."

Good, good, if Khan thinks so, it must be good.

"We are so proud of our Zoe," my father says out of nowhere. "She's our only daughter, you know, and so talented. When she dances, I . . ."

Miraculously, a voice interrupts us. Iris Berrens is

speaking to the gathering. I am so relieved to hear her voice.

"Ladies and gentlemen," she says. "First, we want to thank you so much for being here . . ."

"Have you seen my parents?"

Vic is suddenly standing in front of me. I brace myself.

"Vic, I'm sorry, I have bad news. Your parents couldn't come. Something came up at the last minute and . . ."

"They didn't come!" Vic cries, forgetting to whisper.

People turn their heads and look at us.

"They didn't come?" she repeats, whispering this time.

The expression on her face is hard to read. Even though I know her so well, I can't tell if she's going to burst out laughing or crying.

"They didn't come."

Iris Berrens is still talking. "One of our students will now present a dance he composed himself," she says. "Please join me in the auditorium."

He composed himself? That's a bit of a stretch about Tom. He should clarify that I choreographed the whole thing. I'm about to whisper this to Vic, but she has disappeared. Oh no! She must be so disappointed. I have to find her. I can't leave her alone when she's so upset. I know it won't be the same, but I'm happy to share my parents with her.

"Vic . . ."

Just as I'm about to follow my friend, my mother takes me by the arm and pulls me toward her.

"Wait, Mom, I have to go get Vic . . ."

"Hurry, Sweetie," my mother insists. "Let's go to the auditorium and see the show. Isn't he a friend of yours? You've always made friends so easily. Is he a good dancer?"

What should I do? Do I ditch my mother . . . or Vic? I think about it quickly. It's as if I have a mini Zoe on each of my shoulders. I listen to them both.

MINI ZOE #1: Go after Vic. She has always been there for you. She's your friend. Friendship is sacred.

MINI ZOE #2: You haven't seen your parents for a long time. Two whole months. And you won't see them again for a long time. They came all this way. You can talk to Vic later.

MINI ZOE #1: But it's times like these when you have to recognize . . .

"Oh, Zoe, it's so wonderful to see you again," my father says, putting his arm around my shoulder.

I hug him back and walk toward the auditorium. I'll never know the rest of Mini Zoe #1's advice.

Find Vic!

We settle into the red velvet seats of the auditorium. My father sits on my left, my mother on my right. It reminds me of being at the movies when I was little.

When we entered, I saw Lena with her parents. There was also a boy with them. I wonder who it is. If it's her brother, why hasn't Lena ever mentioned him? Anyway, he's a cute guy. Totally Vic's type. The weird thing is, none of them smile. Not the boy. Not her father and mother. Not Lena. In fact, Lena looks nothing like herself. Maybe it's because her hair is parted down the middle, but I think the real reason is that she's scowling. And then she sits up perfectly straight in her blue skirt and white blouse. I would have liked to keep watching, but they take seats in the back row.

On stage, Iris Berrens announces:

"Please welcome Thomas Muller!"

"Is he a good dancer?" my mother asks me.

"Shhh!"

What else can I say? I can't tell her what I really think about Tom's dancing.

Iris Berrens sits down. Tom makes his entrance.

Smashing! Tom is illuminated by the stage lights. His outfit is fantastic—I hardly recognize him. He's wearing a striped black and white shirt and a bowler hat. Very classy! He looks just like the famous mime, Marcel Marceau. I suddenly have a feeling that Tom will do very well. He'll put on a good show for the parents. And he'll even impress Iris Berrens. Go, Tom! I believe in you! And when you've finished, please give me credit for my choreography.

The music starts.

Tom begins to dance . . . but what is he doing? He shakes all over, brushes his arms, and rocks on his feet. He seems to have forgotten that he's doing steps at all. His hat falls off. He stops, but the music continues, of course. I glance at Iris Berrens. Her eyebrows are knitted. I feel pain at every move. The parents hardly move. They seem frozen. Iris must be getting upset. Everyone knows about her anxiety about the school's reputation, especially since the episode of the health inspection. Now that was a drama in action. Philippe Kauffman turns to her and whispers a few words in her ear. She does not open her mouth. The audience, including the famous Philippe Kauffman, is not sure what to think. Maybe this isn't a serious performance.

Then, with empty eyes, Tom looks at everyone. A few people begin to chuckle. He seems to come back to life, picking up his hat and putting it on his head. He takes an exaggeratedly deep breath and begins to dance. It's worse than ever. He stumbles. He sweats. He tries to arabesque. He completely misses! Abruptly, the music stops.

It seems to be a total disaster, but the audience loves it. Tom is still on stage, glancing around in bewilderment. Then he snaps his fingers and runs to the side of the stage. He lifts a large sign and holds it triumphantly above his head.

Be a Groove High Believer!
Wait Till You See Us in Spring!

Someone in the audience attempts timid applause, and then everyone claps loudly. Grandly, Tom bows and exits offstage.

What a performance!

Iris Berrens coughs and takes the stage.

"I hope you enjoyed Thomas Muller's attempt at . . . entertainment. As you can see, our freshmen are diamonds in the rough. But you can trust that all of the teachers at Groove High are ready to accept the challenge."

How humiliating! And what should I do now? Do I dare tell Philippe Kauffman that I'm a freshman? He'll think we're all like Tom!

My mother whispers in my ear. "What a strange dance! I didn't think you were into experimental dancing at Groove High, but it was pretty cool. I'm just wowed by the creativity . . ."

WHANG, TWANGGGGGGG.

Everyone jumps as a blast of wildly amplified rock music breaks over the school's sound system. I'm scared that Dad has bumped into the controls on the public address system, but he's still sitting next to me. Everyone in the auditorium covers their ears and looks around. Why is this happening today? It's not Friday the 13th. Iris Berrens, along with some of the other teachers, lead the parents toward the exit. Khan goes to the back of the auditorium. Suddenly the distorted guitar sounds stop and the strains of soft violin music float in the air.

"It's just a mistake," he announces.

"A switched disk."

Just a mistake? This makes no sense. As I stand in the crowd, a hand slips into mine. Kevin, Ed's little brother. He smiles at me, blue eyes sparkling.

I'm suspicious. "What happened, Kevin?" I ask.

Kevin gives me a sweet, angelic smile.

"It was cool, right?" he asks.

"What do you mean? Did you . . ."

"Yup. I switched that music myself!"

He is one hundred percent unaware that he has done anything wrong.

"I grabbed one of Ed's heavy metal CDs, snuck into the control room, and, and . . . boy, did you see everyone jump?!"

I don't want to hear any more. I grab him by the shoulders, ready to lecture. But I don't have time before he wraps his little arms around me in a hug.

"I'm glad you're here," he says sweetly. "You're my favorite."

A part of me thinks he's a little brat. But another part of me thinks he's adorable. Kevin, you might be able to get away with anything!

"Can I hang out with you?"

I sigh.

"Okay, but no more pranks, all right?"

"I promise," he says, batting his eyelashes.

He's too cute.

But I still have other things on my mind. Vic has disappeared and thinks her parents don't care about her, and Tom has fled. He's worried that even though he entertained the audience, he didn't impress his classmates. Also, Lena has changed her personality, my mother is talking loudly to anyone who'll listen, my father might spill water all over somebody else, and I still need to find a way to approach Philippe Kauffman. Actually, Kevin might come in handy with the last item on my list.

Wait, where did he go? He let go of my hand, and . . . oh no, he has run off. What mischief will he be up to next?

Oh well, back to the other things, in order of priority. I can't bother about Tom. He'll recover on his own. Maybe he's already started to laugh about the whole situation. As for Lena, I can always just ask her what's going on. But Vic worries me. She's the only freshman whose parents didn't come. Except maybe Kim, but I'm sure they probably went somewhere together.

My mother shakes me out of my thoughts.

"Sweetie, show us around your school! Your father and I want to see it! I'm sure it's amazing. Right, Henry?"

My father nods his head. He nods to almost anything my mother suggests. It's an excellent strategy—he knows any disagreement would be pointless. If he tried to argue, she would never listen.

My mother keeps talking. "First, I want to see your room. You're crazy about decorating. I'm so eager to see it. Did you put up posters?"

I don't respond. My mom just gave me the perfect

excuse to talk to Lena. I have to check with her before I take my parents up to our room. After all, the room isn't just mine. I'll ask Lena if she has hidden Paco somewhere. I can't imagine my mother if she saw Lena's chameleon. Actually, Mom would probably just say "awesome!"

With luck, I'll find Vic in the room and she can finish the tour of the school with us. Where's Lena? Oh, there she is. Her brother looks like a really nice guy—that is, if he is her brother. I don't know who else it could be. He looks a lot like Lena. Lucky for Luke Vandenberg, this boy doesn't go to Groove High. He'd be great competition for Luke. It's strange that Lena has never talked about him to the Groove Team.

"Hey, Lena!"
Only her brother turns to look. Lena stands so straight that it looks like she swallowed a broomstick. Her parents have the same posture. I call again:
"Lena!"
Her brother nudges her with his elbow and points a finger at me. Lena looks over, and her cheeks turn

red. I tell my mother I'll be right back, and I walk over to Lena's family.

"Hello, everyone. I'm Lena's roommate. My name is Zoe."

Her mother looks at me, eyebrows arched. She turns to Lena.

"Helena, make formal introductions, if you please."

Helena? Lena's real name is Helena? My friend chews on the inside of her cheek. It's strange, seeing her without her ever-present bandana on her head.

"Yes, mother," she says in an icy voice. "This is Zoe Myer. Zoe, this is my mother and father, Mr. and Mrs. Robertson, and my brother Yael."

The old Lena is barely recognizable as she says these solemn words.

Mrs. Robertson shakes my hand.

"A pleasure to meet you, Miss Myer."

"Uh, me too, ma'am."

I never imagined Lena's parents like this. Actually, I never imagined them at all, but still . . . Lena is so cool, with her cargo pants, her bandana, her skater shoes, her fluorescent tops. And she never uses such formal language or acts so elegant. In fact, what makes Lena Lena is her completely down to earth attitude! I'm not sure I like this sudden change. Has she been abducted by aliens? Or implanted with Kim's brain? What a scary thought. But no, it's none of these things. Her parents don't seem at all surprised at her behavior. As I'm about to speak again, Iris Berrens appears. I was so distracted by Lena's family, I didn't even notice her walk up.

"Mr. and Mrs. Robertson?"

Iris Berrens extends her hand to Lena's mother, who takes it limply.

"Mrs. Berrens?"

"Yes, I am the director of the school."

"We exchanged a few letters, did we not?"

"That's correct."

I feel cold sweat dripping down my back. This conversation makes me think of vampires! Eek!

"I'm delighted to meet you, Mrs. Berrens," Mrs. Robertson resumes. "We have heard nothing but positive things about your institution, and we rely completely on the discipline of the school to train our Helena in proper manners. She has a tendency not to conform to rules. Isn't that right, Helena?"

Lena has not even looked at her mother. I can see

she is about to explode. I feel like I've entered another dimension.

"Helena?" Mrs. Robertson insists.

I must do something.

"Um, pardon me. I need to speak to Lena for a minute. I have to ask her if . . . um . . . if the room is . . ."

Lena stares at me, looking panicked. No, no, don't worry, Lena. I've never even heard the word *chameleon*. Anyway, her parents don't seem to notice me. They're deep in conversation with Iris Berrens. Even better. Now I can talk to Lena.

"Hey, are you okay? Is there something I can do?"

Lena shakes her head. It looks like her teeth are glued together. Suddenly, her brother, Yael—I had not noticed he was dressed in cool gray pants and a jacket with gold buttons—looks at me.

"Hey, who is this beauty?"

Then his eyes slide away from me. I follow them. Vic has just walked past us, moving fast. Her eyes are red. Obviously, she's upset about her parents. I should go to her. Her words still ring in my ears: *I thought friends were supposed to support each other!*

"Lena, who is she?" Lena's brother says, staring at Vic as she disappears in the crowd.

I reply by calling out to her.

"Vic!"

Yael follows me as I try to chase her. He glances at his parents, then whispers, "Be sure to tell her I think she's cute."

I don't like this at all. Sorry about your brother, Lena, but he seems like a jerk. I'll bet he thinks he can just snap his fingers and have whatever he wants. Maybe his parents do, too. If Lena didn't look so much like them, I'd swear she was adopted.

I have to find Vic. I look around, but she's gone from sight again. What's going on? She's like a secret agent today.

"Ladies and gentlemen," Khan announces pleasantly. "Refreshments are now being served in the cafeteria. Please come and meet the rest of the teachers at Groove High."

My parents! I'd almost forgotten about them. Once again, I'm torn. Vic or them? What a tough call. But there's always an answer—just think!—yes, that's it! I'll go with Mom and Dad to the cafeteria, let them talk to the teachers, and while they're busy chatting, I'll disappear. Mission: Find Vic! And don't forget Tom, either. Until just now, I hadn't thought about him.

A Quick Getaway

"**E**eeeeeeeek!"

A piercing cry rings out in the cafeteria. What's happening? A fire? A murder? Everyone stops in place and looks around.

A lady in a pale blue suit stares at her cake as if it's going to attack her. Her eyes bug out an inch from her head. As I come closer, I see that there is a huge spider on the creamy white icing. It's hairy, like those spiders from the Amazon—poisonous spiders!

Kevin!

I see him hiding behind a column. He wouldn't miss this show for anything. I go over and grab him by the collar.

"Hey!"

"What did you do now, Kevin? Did you sneak this spider into Groove High?"

"Isn't it freaky?" he says. "I bought it at the toy store in the mall! I have to get it back. It looks so real!"

I roll my eyes. He's a hopeless little twerp. A small group of parents and students gather around the distraught woman. A large man, who seems to be her husband, taps her on the hand and shows her that the spider is just plastic. Kevin is proud of his latest victory. The commotion calms down gradually. I know what I have to do. I will drag this little trouble-maker to his father. I can't complain. It gives me the perfect chance to talk to my idol in person.

"Follow me, Kevin."

The troublemaker doesn't argue. He takes me by the hand. Just like a professional actor, he now changes into a perfectly innocent-looking, well-mannered little boy. Philippe Kauffman is talking with Iris Berrens; he hasn't left her side since the beginning of the afternoon. He's loud. I'm not very close to him, and I can still hear everything he says.

"Your school is charming, Iris. Really. But what a shame that you don't have any stars in this year."

I'm stunned. How can he say this? What does he know about our year? He knows that Tom was a disaster, but Tom's just one student.

"Indeed, it is increasingly difficult to find a star!" he goes on. "Do you remember when we were studying together in New York? We worked twenty-four hours a day! This is the only way to become the best. Young people today don't have that drive! I see this in my own school and even with my own son, if you'll permit me to say. He tries, but he doesn't give enough of himself."

What? How can he say that we're lazy? What does he know about how I work? Or how Vic and Lena work? Above all, how dare he say that Ed, his own son, doesn't give enough of himself? Every night, Ed spends at least two hours practicing in the dance studio!

What about his Friday evening and Saturday practices? Ed works so much that he has to be careful not to burn himself out.

Iris Berrens looks at Philippe and gently shakes her head. I hope this puts him in his place.

Wishful thinking.

"You know what I prefer, Philippe?" she says, almost in a whisper. "Patience, hope, and faith. Some of these young people will blossom into stars like I was, or choreographers like you. I'm convinced that they will inspire audiences."

Suddenly, my excitement fades. For my entire life, I have dreamed of speaking with this man, and now that I am actually in front of him, I have lost all desire to be here.

And then I see that Kevin is gone.

"Honey? Is that you there?"

My parents found me! My dad's mouth is full of creamed cabbage. He even has some on his cheek. Creamed cabbage has always been his guilty pleasure.

"So you'll take us to your room now?" asks my mother giddily. "I want to know all about your world! I lived in dorms, too, and hung out with my girlfriends. We totally rocked! Of course, we were always crazy about the boys!" She throws back her head and laughs. "It was a blast!"

I had not thought about this part. If I take Mom to our dorm room and find Vic in full depression mode, she will see it as the opportunity of a lifetime. I can picture every detail. While Dad wanders about, breaking everything in the place, Mom sits next to Vic and tries to console her. She'll ask nosy questions. She'll tell Vic about what she did when she was our age. And after asking enough questions and telling enough stories, Mom will have to come to one conclusion: Vic is suffering from a broken heart. At this point, there's no turning back. Mom will try to discover the name of the boy who hurt Vic and deliver her a long, wise lecture. She'll tell Vic how some boys are like this, and that she can't blame them, but she also can't let them lead her on.

No. I can't put Vic through that. She is my best friend, after all. So I exclaim, trying to be as cheery as possible:

"Not just yet! We should visit the park first! You'll see—it's so great!"

The park is so big that we probably won't bump into other parents. Then my dad won't break anything. Which is perfect! Mom isn't thrilled.

"The park? Leave the school? Well, if you think so, I guess it's okay."

I knew she'd go along in the end. We leave and

head toward the park.

"There it is!"

I'm about to make a quick getaway, when . . .

"Hello. You must be Zoe's parents. Mr. and Mrs. Myer, correct?"

My blood freezes in my veins.

"I imagine that your daughter has told you about me. My name is Miss Nakamura, and I am in charge of discipline at this institution."

"Uh, no," my dad says without thinking.

Miss Nakamura frowns. "Indeed, your daughter does give me a few problems at times. I feel compelled to inform you that she, along with a few other students, have formed a small, shall I say, clique—that I keep my eye on. You see, I am especially observant of certain groups of young people."

Miss Nakamura makes me sound like a juvenile delinquent.

"It is not for lack of examples to follow," she says. "Kimberly Vandenberg is a perfect example. I wish every student could be as well behaved as she is. Recently . . ."

"Mr. and Mrs. Myer, I presume?"

I had to force my eyes open because I was squeezing them shut so tightly. It is Mr. Carter, our music teacher, and he is saving my life. He's one of those people whose age is impossible to pin down. He might be 45 years old . . .or 250. He has a black beard streaked with patches of gray hair, and is always dressed in a frock coat with tails—both old and frayed. To complete his outfit, he wears a top hat! He's wearing it right now, and he bows and greets my parents by lifting the hat a little.

"I'm Eric Carter. I teach music here to all the students. I'm always happy to meet parents!"

Miss Nakamura lets out sigh before going to meet other parents. I'm not worried about her, though. She won't run out of acid to add to every word she utters. Just like Kim, her favorite. Whatever. I listen to what Mr. Carter tells my parents. You know, he kind of looks rumpled and old, but he's totally into of the latest trends in music. He's even managed to impress Tom, who no one can beat when it comes to the music scene.

Mom and Dad look a bit bewildered listening to him. I'm pretty sure they have no clue what he's talking about. Meanwhile, Miss Gaultier is chatting with other parents. I wave at her. I love Miss Gaultier, the choreography instructor. You may have heard of her. She choreographed many famous ballets, including *The Bad Moons* and *The Semaphore*, all of which were performed at the Grand Contemporary Ballet Festival in Montreal. She has also collaborated with a lot of famous musicians. She developed dance moves for Threatz, the rapper, and for Jadon Ramirez, the singer. She is as strict as Iris Berrens, but she leaves her students with a better feeling. With Miss Gaultier, I don't always feel like the biggest screw-up on earth. Now, I hope she will stop to talk to my parents. Choreography is my best class. I'm beginning to feel bad that Mom is stuck with Mr. Carter. But maybe she's lucky. She could be stuck with Miss Cohen, our math teacher. That would definitely be worse. All she talks about are functions and equilateral triangles. Do you know what those are? Don't worry, me neither. In class, she makes jokes about Newton and Euclid that only she laughs at. Crazy!

My mother gives me a look that says "I want to tell you something." Then I notice that Luke is only a few feet away from me. Oh no. He wouldn't dare. Not now, not in front of parents, and not my parents!

He looks at me.

My mother watches. Luke and I lock eyes. He takes a step toward us. Stop that smiling, Luke. And then he winks!

After that, he turns and leaves.

My mother takes me by the arm and squeezes it as if it's an orange, and she wants the juice.

"Who was that cool guy? Is he your boyfriend? Tell me, Zoe—are you going out with him? Tell me! After all, Zoe, I'm not just your mother. I'm your best friend."

Help!

Upside Down

My entire world is collapsing around me.

So there I was, trying to escape my mother's interrogation techniques. If she had her way, she'd burn me at the stake, or stretch me out on the rack, or put me in an iron maiden, all to find out more about Luke. I had already told her that he was not my boyfriend, or even a friend. I hated him. But the more I tried to explain that he was the most pretentious boy in school, that he was not my style, and that his sister was my sworn enemy, the more it encouraged her. "Oh! It's so sweet! So romantic!" she purred.

My dad, meanwhile, wanted a tour of the school. He wouldn't take no for an answer. He just marched through doorways with comments like "this is beautiful!" and "would you look at that!" and "now, that's interesting!" I managed to tear myself away from Mom long enough to answer some of his questions: "That's a classroom, Dad. Yes, and that one is, too. No, no! Not that! That's . . .the girls' bathroom." Too late. He already went in. I had to follow him.

And, of course, guess who's in the girls' bathroom. Who else would stand there appalled? Who else would scream, as if we had burst in on her taking a shower when she's really only putting on her make-up in front of the mirror?

Kim. So she wasn't out with her parents eating sushi. She'd probably rather be in here staring at her own reflection, anyway.

In any case, she was there at that very moment, staring at my dad with complete and utter fury. Slowly, she opened her mouth . . .

I grabbed my dad by the sleeve and yanked him out of the bathroom. Kim decided to follow. I didn't know what to expect at that moment. She came close and gave me a friendly hug. I was totally shocked until she whispered in my ear:

"So these are your parents, Myer? This explains a lot." She smiled as she turned to go back into the bathroom. If Vic were here, she wouldn't hesitate to say something like: "I'm so happy that they finally found a dorm room for you! It's so perfectly Kim!" Too bad I thought of this ten seconds after Kim had left—an eternity later. While I silently wondered why Kim's parents had not shown up, my father exclaimed:

"Your friend is so charming! She seems like a very nice girl."

That's it. I had no choice. I had to get rid of my parents. Somehow. I led them back to the cafeteria where we met Miss Cohen. Remember Miss Cohen, my single-minded math teacher? She lives in her perfect alternate universe of formulas and equations. I introduced my parents to her, and as I expected, she began the lecture on math. I know, I know. I'm a rude daughter. True, the solution to my problem was cruel and unusual, but this was a matter of life and death. (As in: my own death. If Mom continued to pester me about Luke, and if Dad said one more nice thing about Kim, I think I would have jumped off the roof of Groove High.)

I took the opportunity to disappear. I had to find Vic and Tom. I imagined them along with everyone else desperately hiding in a corner. As I crossed the lobby, I heard voices. I listened in—yes, I know about being polite, but I can't help myself! It's second nature! As I listened, I figured out that I wasn't hearing voices, but a voice: Philippe Kauffman's

voice. I crept closer. He was surrounded by a group of parents who were completely captivated by a story of his experience dining at an exclusive restaurant. It was like a one-man show.

Suddenly, it hit me. This man, who was my lifelong hero and the reason I wanted to be a choreographer, was a normal person! I had to face it. Philippe Kauffman had some traits that were not very attractive. Of course, I expected him to be elegant and worldly. But I didn't expect him to be so into himself. After listening to him, I saw that he seemed to eat, breathe, and live one thing: Philippe Kauffman. My hero had faults. Faults . . . like everyone has. I took a deep breath. For years, when I thought of Philippe Kauffman, I felt I could soar like an eagle. Now I wondered. Maybe I was just a silly duck.

That was when I spotted Ed. He was sitting on a bench in the hall. I waved at him, but he only responded with a gloomy nod. I sat down next to him without saying anything. He really didn't need to tell me how difficult it was for him. Being the son of Philippe Kauffman meant being in the shadow of a man who was always the center of attention.

Having a famous father wasn't enough. Ed needed a father to encourage him, not publicly criticize him and call him lazy. I knew what Ed wanted: a father who took care of him, who asked questions about school, friends, teachers, classes. The way my parents do.

"Come with me," I urged him. "I'm trying to find Vic and Tom."

He shook his head and pointed to his brother, Kevin, playing hopscotch on the tiles. Kevin was uncharacteristically well behaved.

"I need to keep an eye on Kevin. You know, he might blow up Groove High or burn it down or something."

I smiled as I stood up.

"Call if you need me, okay?"

Then I left. I had a mission to accomplish.

First step: try to get them on their cell phones. Vic's phone went straight to voice mail. Tom's too. Oh, well. Looked like I was back to the good, old-fashioned way of finding people. I walked over to the east wing of the school, to the girls' dorms. When I reached our dorm room, I stopped. I could hear people fighting behind the door. I could make out Lena's voice. Were she and Vic going at it again over Paco?

"Helena, this is outrageous! You cannot live here!" a female voice cried out.

It wasn't Vic.

"Stop it, Mother!" Lena yelled back. "I love it here! I share this room with my friends! Vic and Zoe are the best! Please don't make me get a single!"

That was true. Vic and I are the best.

"We will spare no expense," said a male voice. "We'll donate more to the school."

"Father, stop!" said Lena in a strangled voice. "Donations are not the solution. You're not listening!"

"Don't you dare talk that way to us!" cried Mrs. Robertson. "Maybe this school is teaching you the wrong things, Helena."

"Maybe you're right, Mom!" screamed Lena. "First of all, no one here calls me Helena. It's Lena! And I never wear these weird clothes! I wear sweats and a bandana on my head!"

"Well!" Lena's mother was stunned.

"They love me for who I am here! Not because we're wealthy and have influence in this city!"

I didn't need a set of instructions to tell me that this was not a good time to enter. In any case, Vic was obviously not there.

I find an empty study room and sit down to think. I'm sitting there now. It is a relief to be alone. With my entire world collapsing around me, I need a moment to think straight.

Vic has disappeared. Tom, too. Philippe Kauffman is no longer my idol, and Lena's real name is Helena.

I feel a little dizzy.

Suddenly, a few notes playing on a guitar catch my ear. How beautiful! Whoever is strumming now breaks out into a rich Spanish melody. I close my eyes for a moment and imagine myself in a field full of purple bougainvilleas, with a fountain and pool that glisten in the sun . . .

I open my eyes to find myself back in the study room. I leave to find out who is playing. Then the music stops. Oh no! How will I find out who was playing those soulful notes? Wait! Now I hear a girl's voice.

The music starts again. It sounds very different. In

fact, I know this song. It's BlueDay! They're a rock group from L.A. This guitar player is really good! I continue to follow the sounds, and after a little bit,

it stops again. I hear another voice. Tom! I think his voice is coming from another empty study room. Maybe he's hiding out there, like I was. I don't think he's alone so I push open the door to the room, taking care not to make noise, and look inside.

It is Tom. His back is to the door. And he isn't alone. And I would have never guessed the person with him.

The Inside Stories

Neither Tom nor his companion moves. They are sitting very close to each other, talking intently together. They don't hear me. I freeze, both to keep quiet and because I am totally shocked.

It's Tom and Vic! I have spent my entire afternoon looking for them, and here they are together, far away from everyone!

I can't believe my eyes! But I don't think I'm dreaming. Vic, who usually treats Tom like dirt, has her head on his shoulder. Tom has his guitar resting on his knees. I knew that he had a guitar, but I had never heard him actually play it. I sort of figured that he didn't know how. But was I wrong. He's a virtuoso!

"That one was amazing," says Vic.

Did I just hear Vic compliment Tom? Now I'm sure that I'm in some bizarro world. I can't keep my jaw from dropping as I hear every word they say to each other. They think they're alone. I keep listening:

Tom (shrugging, with a soft, ironic laugh): I know. If there's one thing I can do, it's play the guitar. I wish I could do more than one thing well, though.

Vic (assuring—and no, I'm not kidding): You are not just good at one thing. I mean, you're using your talent here at Groove High, right? You should stop beating yourself up.

Tom (now breathing a long sigh): Before Groove High, I was in a music conservatory. I liked it well enough, but it was boring. I wanted to do something different.

Wow! I never imagined I'd be hearing this from Tom. He sounds serious instead of silly. There's so much disappointment in his voice.

Tom (still somber): Look how that turned out. I'm not very good at this. You saw the show.

Vic (laughing, perhaps to ease the tension): It wasn't so bad.

Tom (suddenly): I'm leaving Groove High.

Vic gasps.

Vic: I think you're overreacting.

Tom: No. I don't think so. In fact, I think I'm reacting the right amount. How could I ever think I could be a dancer?

Vic (now totally serious, and kind of bossy): You can't leave Groove High! The year isn't even done yet! We've barely begun! Why can't you be a dancer?

There's the Vic I know!

Tom: Thanks, but I know how it is. I'm a horrible dancer. I'm more like a clown. I know that people laugh at me behind my back. You were right this morning. Groove High is a school, not a circus. I . . .

Vic: Forget about what I said this morning!

I was super anxious and felt like throwing up! This parent thing is really bothering me.

Tom: Why?

Silence. Vic slouches lower in her seat.

Tom (insistent): Why are you worried? Didn't you just say that your parents weren't . . .

Vic: Exactly.

I'm still frozen. I can't do anything but listen. Vic's earlier words to me play back in my mind on more time: *I thought friends were supposed to support each other*! What was she trying to tell me?

Vic (her voice little more than a whimper): I didn't want them to come.

Silence again.

Vic: I didn't think they would fit in. Not at Groove High.

Tom: I don't understand.

But I think I do understand what my best friend is saying.

Vic: My dad and mom work hard and love me. But they look at life differently. They don't really understand what I'm learning here. They think that I'm just wasting my time, that when I get older, I'll finally be "normal." You know—I'll get married, get a job.

They don't think studying to be a dancer is going to help me make it in the "real world." You know?

Her voice breaks.

She's right. About all of it. Now, I know Vic's parents. I love them. They are wonderful, generous people. But they don't think Vic's talent is important. They don't understand why she spends her time dancing, why she is so passionate about being the best she can be. It makes her so frustrated. I guess that's where she gets the motivation to succeed. She wants to prove her parents wrong. Hearing Vic, I start thinking about my mom and dad. They pay for me to be at Groove High. They're not rich, but they support me. Vic is here on a scholarship. She babysits to pay for her computer and her clothes. She always drives herself to excel. And she does! She performs better than everyone else.

That's why I thought that she'd want her parents to see her. I thought that she'd be so proud to show them everything she'd accomplished. Suddenly, I realize that I don't understand a lot about my best friend. I frown. I'm not very proud of the friend I've been.

Vic (looking straight ahead): So, imagine my surprise when they decide to skip Parents' Day!

Vic (sighs): I wish they could understand.

My mind is racing right now. I never knew how Vic felt. And I had no idea about Tom. In fact, Lena's whole situation went under my radar, and I just left Ed to brood over his self-important father. I promise myself right now that I'll be a better friend. While I'm at it, I'll be a better daughter, too. It doesn't matter that I have to put up with my mom's overgrown-kid style, and that my dad is kind of absent-minded. They are there for me, and they love me. They have always stood by me, and I know that they always will. I decide that I'm going to start now.

I have to find them.

I walk up the hallway back toward the lobby and cafeteria. I'm basically running. But when I turn a corner, I literally run into Luke.

Luke, who grabs me by the shoulders to stop me from falling, who smiles at me, who, for once, does not call me "Carrot Top."

Picking Up the Pieces

Sorry!

I avoid Luke's gaze and try to sneak past him. But he's able to stop me.

"What's the hurry, Zoe?"

He called me Zoe. How does he know my name?

"I . . . I'm going to the cafeteria," I stammer. "My parents are there, and I'm late meeting up with them."

Wait a minute. Why am I even explaining this to Luke? I must not be thinking straight. He's just going to twist what I say into more insults and more names. He thinks I'm nothing but an annoying freshman.

"Yeah, I saw them talking with Miss Genet."

Miss Genet is the school librarian. She and I get along well. I figure she'll say some nice things about me. She and my parents are probably talking about how she helped us with our magazine.

"Really? Miss Genet? After we released the first issue of the *Groove Zine*, we asked her if we could get new books for the reference section so we could use them as resources. She set aside a whole computer terminal loaded with software and even a drawing tablet. She really went all out for us!"

"Oh."

I have just said more to Luke than I have in the entire time I've known him. I blush, and then I'm confused. What's going on? I want to slap myself.

Luke just looks at me.

"Something wrong, Carrot Top?"

There! I knew it was coming!

Except that Luke doesn't seem to be insulting me this time. He sounds different. Sweet. And kind. I don't know what to say. I shrug in response. Wait a second—am I crying? I feel the stinging in my eyes, and there are definitely tears. I am crying. Yes, that's correct. A huge tear rolls down the side of my nose and hesitates for a second before dripping off and falling onto my shoe.

"Is something wrong?" he asks me in a soft voice.

I shake my head. I'm not lying. I don't know why I'm crying! Maybe nerves? This day has been way too emotional.

Luke leads me to a bench and makes me sits down. Then he sits next to me. He starts to talk.

"I know you admire him a lot. Philippe Kauffman, I mean."

I don't know what I'm hearing. He knows my name, he knows who my parents are, he knows that I idolize Philippe Kauffman. Why would he know all these things about a nobody like me?

"I was watching you watching him today."

Luke Vandenberg spent his day spying on me! What is going on? Did he hear how horrible his sister was to me?

"You can't think about what he said," Luke tells me. "Even if he isn't quite the person you thought he was, it doesn't take away from his talent."

How is he doing this? It's like he's reading my mind. It's all true. I do have some doubts about whether or not I should admire Philippe Kauffman. About whether or not I had made a mistake. It is bothering me so much that I am starting to have doubts about becoming a choreographer. In my mind, Philippe Kauffman and his work are on the highest pedestal I can imagine. When I saw him act so vain and pompous, he took a big fall.

"Believe me," says Luke, "it's so important to separate the man and his work. You should admire his inventiveness and imagination. The fact that he has no clue how to raise a son shouldn't take away from those things."

I'm silent and amazed. Luke is the last person I'd expect to have that kind of understanding. I'm not sure I trust him, but his words do make me feel better. In fact, they're exactly what I need. It's as if he stopped my confidence from falling and breaking into pieces.

Then a thought pops into my mind. Kim was alone today. Her parents did not come to school. Why? How long has it been since Luke and Kim have seen their parents?

I shyly raise my eyes to him and attempt a smile. Was I wrong about Luke all this time?

Suddenly, streaks of blue, red, and yellow whoosh past me.

"Hey!" Luke yells as a water balloon bursts directly on his forehead. Two others find their mark on his stomach and shoulders. Dripping water blinds him and he starts rubbing his eyes. A perfect opening! More balloons sail right into the back of his head and neck. Now water is trickling down inside his shirt collar.

"What? Who?"

We hear a gleeful screech. "Mission accomplished!"
This kid did not mean a word he said to me earlier.
Kevin is hysterically laughing and hopping.
"Got you! Oh boy, I got you!"

Luke starts to wipe himself off with his sleeve but quits to chase Kevin. He plans to strangle the boy. It's chaos as Kevin runs from Luke and crashes right into me. He yells:

"Zo-ee! Zo-ee! I'm going to tell everyone that you love Luke!"

Now I'm going to strangle him!

I join the chase. The sooner I catch that genius of a troublemaker the better!

The Inseparable Groove Team

Of course, the chase didn't end there!

I was like an Olympic runner, tearing after the kid down the halls. Kevin had his escape route planned. He dove right into the crowd of parents and teachers, searching for protection. He found it behind his father's long legs. A second later, I arrived. I realized that I was nose-to-nose with Philippe Kauffman! Automatically, I smoothed down my hair and tried not to reveal what I was thinking of doing to his son.

"Zoe!" Dad exclaimed. "We were just talking about you! Do you know who this is? This is Philippe Kauffman! Your idol!"

"As I said," continued Dad, turning to Philippe, "my daughter has worshipped you since she's been able to walk."

My parents were talking to the greatest choreographer alive today. About me. Philippe Kauffman raised his eyebrow and turned his head toward me.

"You want to be a choreographer?"

The words were stuck in my mouth. I couldn't say a thing. So I had no choice but to let the man speak.

"Very good, very good! Never forget one thing: you must always invent, create, and invent some more! Imagination is the most important part of our art form!"

"Oh, invent!" cried my mother. "You don't have to worry there. Zoe is the best at that. When she was little . . ."

I tried my best to block out Mom's embarrassing Baby Zoe story. But whatever! My dream had come true. I was talking to Philippe Kauffman. Honestly, it was more like he talked and I listened. I couldn't forget that he had said "our art form!" Isn't that fabulous?

And that's it. The parents have all left now. The Groove High doors are closed, and everything is back to normal. Believe me, everything is in order:

1. Lena started wearing her bandana and sweats again. They suit her so much better than that pleated skirt.

2. Tom decided to stay at Groove High. Just now, he rushed over to hold a door open for Vic.

3. Ed practices as hard as ever at the ballet barre.

4. Kim was reunited with Clarisse and Angie, her little toadies. They're in town looking for her favorite sushi right now.

5. And finally, I passed by Luke in the hallway ten minutes ago. He ruffled my hair and called me "Carrot Top."

Didn't I tell you?

After their long discussion with Philippe Kauffman, my parents were enthusiastic enough to continue their grand tour of the school. I introduced them to everyone. My mom never stopped talking, and my dad managed to be as awkward as ever. Vic came along for the ride. She had always liked hanging out with my parents. My mom insisted that Vic's parents really did want to come.

Tom also found his parents. I heard him talk

proudly about his time at Groove High. You know me—I couldn't help but listen. When Tom's father asked him whether he'd rather devote his studies to music, Tom stated that he was determined to chase his dreams at Groove High. He loved it more than any other place in the world. As Philippe Kauffman was leaving, I was surprised to hear Iris Berrens tell Philippe what a promising dancer Ed was. Philippe Kauffman said nothing, but I'm pretty sure that he looked proud of his son. The "good-bye" between Lena and her family was frosty. She watched her father, mother, and brother leave, and only smiled after her family climbed into their limo with its black-tinted windows.

Vic, Lena, and I are now in the library writing articles for the next release of *Groove Zine*. It's a special "Parents' Day" issue. We expect Ed and Tom to arrive soon and make the Groove Team complete. Lena has Paco with her. Poor guy. He spent the whole day hiding in the closet in our dorm room. Of course, he had his dried insects, but they don't replace tender loving care. While she plays with her chameleon, Lena talks with Vic about I don't know what. I haven't yet found a good time to talk with her about her parents, but maybe tonight before going to sleep, we'll catch up.

I learned a lot today. About my friends and about myself. I feel like my old beliefs have been shaken up. The Groove Team is as close as ever, but we've had a peek into each other's hidden sides. We definitely aren't the same after these experiences. Vic and I are still close, of course. We've been that way since we were both seven years old. But now I know more about Tom, Ed, Lena—and Vic, too. We're inseparable, and we can always count on each other.

"Hey! Guess what!" Tom says as he bursts into the room.

"What is it?" asks Vic. "Let me guess. You learned how to tie your shoelaces!"

Tom does not laugh. He continues talking:

"Just now, Zach asked me to sign up for Capoeira Club."

Zach is Luke's best friend. Tom is their roommate.

"Wow!" says Lena. "That's pretty cool!"

I don't want to get ahead of myself, but I can't help but wonder.

"Why did he come up with this idea all of a sudden?

Tom smiles wider. "He saw my show this afternoon, and he thinks that I, in his words, 'have a remarkable dancing style that would be perfect for Capoeira!'"

Lena breaks out laughing.

"Remarkable dancing style is right!"

Tom blushes. The memory of his ridiculous performance still stings. But he does not stop smiling.

"So Luke is handling Capoeira Club?" says Vic. "Like, he'll be there. You could introduce me to him!"

The color drains from Tom's face. See? Everything is back to normal. Oh, Tom, don't you see, it's hope-

less! At some point, you'll realize that Vic might not be for you. The strangest thing is that when Vic said Luke's name, I felt this twinge in my stomach. His voice this afternoon. It was so kind and understanding, so . . .

I shake my head. Come on. I have to be normal, too. Remember, he's a big show-off who's with a different girl every other week! Don't forget that he is everything you hate: superficial, pretentious, and most of all, he's Kim's brother!

The door gently opens, and in comes Ed, who quietly sits at the table. He smiles. This is no small feat for him.

Well, here we all are!

Cool! We're ready for whatever comes our way.

Raise the curtain, and let the music begin!

Our School

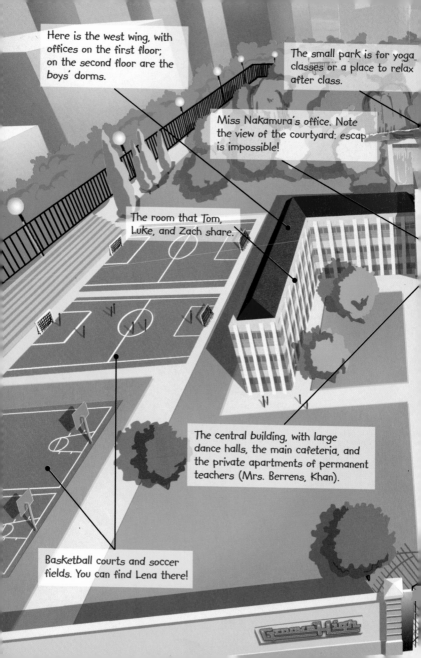

About the Author

Amélie Sarn: Amelie has two major flaws: excessive curiosity and a tendency to gorge herself. Not just on food, but on reading, travel, games, children, friends, and anything that makes her laugh. This gives her lots of material for stories! When her publisher asked her to write the stories of Zoe and the Groove Team, she revealed her dark side. Of all the characters in *Groove High*, she admits that her favorite is Kim!

About the Illustrator

Virgile Trouillot: With his feet on the ground, but his head forever in the clouds, Virgile spent his youth under the constant influence of cartoons, manga, and other comics. When he's not illustrating *Groove High* Books, Virgile develops animated series for *Planet Nemo*. Virgile spends time in his own version of a city zoo that's right in his apartment. His non-human companions include an army of ninja chinchillas that he has raised himself and many insects that science has not yet identified.

Web Sites

In order to ensure the safety and currency of recommended Internet links, Windmill maintains and updates an online list of sites. To access links to learn more about the *Groove High* characters and their adventures, please go to www.windmillbooks.com/weblinks and select this book's title.

For more great fiction and nonfiction, go to www.windmillbooks.com.